Walt Disney's
Mickey Mouse
and the PET SHOW

A Golden Book · New York
Western Publishing Company, Inc.
Racine, Wisconsin 53404

Mickey and his nephews, Morty and Ferdie, were in Mickey's backyard getting ready for a cookout.

"Where's Minnie?" wondered Mickey.

"And the fudge layer cake she promised?" asked the boys.

A minute later, Pluto barked his friendly welcome as Minnie came hurrying through the gate.

"I'm sorry to be late," she said, handing the boys her cake. "I've just been elected chairperson of the Charity Pet Show."

"With you in charge, it's certain to be a success," Mickey said enthusiastically.

"Why, thank you," Minnie said. "I certainly hope so. We have to raise a lot of money to build a brand-new shelter for stray animals."

"Let's enter Pluto in the show!" Morty suggested excitedly.

"But Pluto isn't a show dog," Mickey reminded the boys.

"We can train him!" said Ferdie.

"All right," Mickey agreed, "if it'll help raise money for stray animals."

As soon as the boys had finished their
second helpings of Minnie's cake, they
started to train Pluto for the pet show.

"Roll over, Pluto!" ordered Morty.

But Pluto didn't understand. He sat up
and wagged his tail.

"Maybe we should *show* him what we want," said Ferdie.

Pluto watched, puzzled, as both boys rolled over.

"Let's pick something he *likes* to do," suggested Morty.

So Ferdie ordered, "Lie down, Pluto!"
Instead, Pluto jumped up and began
chasing his tail.

"Look, Minnie!" said Mickey. "The boys have really got him doing things!"

"But they're just not the *right* things," wailed Morty and Ferdie.

All week long, Morty and Ferdie tried to teach Pluto new tricks. He fetched, rolled over, sat up, lay down, and shook hands . . . but only when *he* wanted to.

"He'll be the only pet to fail every test," said Mickey sadly.

On the day of the show, Mickey and the
boys took Pluto to the empty lot next door,
where the show was being held. Minnie
sold Mickey three tickets, then pointed
happily to the cashbox.

"We've got enough money right now to
pay for the animal shelter!" she told him.

"That's great!" said Mickey.

What *wasn't* so great was Pluto's performance that day.

He shook hands when he was told to sit; he rolled over when he should have jumped. He barked when he was supposed to lie down. The audience roared with laughter.

Worst of all, when Police Chief O'Hara was choosing the Best Pet of the Day, Pluto growled at him! The chief didn't know it, but he was standing on the very spot where Pluto had buried a good bone!

Suddenly screams were heard from the
ticket booth. "Help! Stop, thief! Help!"

"That's Minnie!" Mickey gasped.

"The ticket money!" yelped the boys, and
Chief O'Hara led the way to the booth.

Pluto was already at the scene of the crime when the others got there. He was busily sniffing around the booth.

"I'm all right, Mickey," Minnie said, "but the money is gone. When I came back to get it, I saw someone running away with the cashbox."

"What did the robber look like?" asked the chief.

"I don't know," Minnie replied. "I didn't see his face."

"Which way did he go?" Mickey asked.

Just then, before Minnie could answer,
Pluto took off for the woods.

"He's tracking the thief!" shouted Mickey. "Go, Pluto!"

"It's more likely that he's tracking a
pussycat," snorted Chief O'Hara.

But it was no pussycat that ran scream-ing out of the woods. It was the thief—hanging on to the cashbox and followed by Pluto, who was clenching his teeth on the thief's suspenders!

"Save me!" yelled the thief.

S-s-snap! went his suspenders, shooting him right into Chief O'Hara's arms.

Later, at police headquarters, Chief O'Hara presented Pluto with the Four-Footed Hero Award.

The chief smiled. "Thanks to Pluto, animals who are lost will have a shelter and a chance to find good homes."

On the way to Mickey's house, Morty proudly announced, "Pluto's better than a show dog. He's a *hero* dog."

Suddenly Pluto barked a sharp warning.

"Ferdie!" shouted Mickey, pulling him back to the curb. "Didn't you see that car?"

"Pluto did," said Minnie, patting him.

As they started to cross the street, an old man dropped his cane.

With a friendly wag of his tail, Pluto picked up the cane and gave it back to him.

"That's a nice dog you have," the old man said to Mickey, and they all watched, smiling, as Pluto bounded on ahead.

When they got to Mickey's house, Pluto
was waiting on the doorstep. He wagged
his tail and barked his friendly welcome.

"Do you know what, boys?" said Mickey happily. "Who cares whether Pluto wins prizes or is a hero? He's everybody's friend —and that's what counts!"

Minnie and Morty and Ferdie agreed. Pluto shook hands with everyone because *this* was a time when *he* wanted to—and because he was the happiest of them all!